I AM SO ANGRY, I COULD
SCREAM

Helping Children Deal with Anger

by Laura Fox, MA
Illustrated by Chris Sabatino

New Horizon Press
Far Hills, New Jersey

Copyright © 2000 by Laura Fox
Illustrated by Chris Sabatino

All rights reserved. No portion of this book may be reproduced or transmitted in any form
whatsoever, including electronic, mechanical or any information storage or retrieval system,
except as may be expressly permitted in the 1976 Copyright Act or in writing from the publisher.

Requests for permission should be addressed to:
New Horizon Press
P.O. Box 669
Far Hills, NJ 07931

Laura Fox
    I Am So Angry, I Could Scream: Helping Children Deal with Anger

Cover Design and Interior Illustrations: Chris Sabatino

Library of Congress Control Number: 00-132570

ISBN-10 (paperback): 0-88282-185-7
ISBN-13 (paperback): 978-0-88282-185-6

SMALL HORIZONS
A Division of New Horizon Press

Printed in the U.S.A.

19   18   17   3   4   5   6

All around the schoolyard are candy wrappers, paper cups and bits of uneaten food.

"Gross!" Penny calls out to her friend as she steps on a rotten apple and slides. She almost falls but catches herself.

"Penny, are you hurt?" asks Patty, Penny's best friend.

"I am okay," Penny replies, brushing herself off. "Look at all this trash. I do not know why people throw their garbage on the ground. There is a trash can just a few feet away." Penny frowns, looking around.

"I know! I cannot believe how lazy some people are," agrees Patty.

"Some people act like pigs and it really makes me mad," states Penny. "In fact, it makes me so angry, I could scream."

As Penny and Patty walk to class, a third girl, Dianne, joins them.

"Hi, Penny! Hi, Patty!" Dianne says.

"Hi, Dianne," the girls answer at the same time.

Dianne stares at Penny. "Penny, you wear that yellow sweater too much. It is yucky." Dianne points to Penny's favorite sweater. "It makes you look like a rubber duck!" Dianne begins to laugh.

Penny feels tears come to her eyes. Although Penny and Dianne are supposed to be friends, Dianne often says mean things to Penny about her hair or her clothes. This really upsets Penny. Penny feels so angry that she could scream, but she keeps quiet.

"Are you coming to my party at the ice skating rink next Saturday?" Dianne asks. "My parents are going to drop us off, but they are not going to hang around. We will be able to do whatever we want for once," Dianne brags.

"I do not know. I have not asked my parents yet," Patty says.

"I have not asked my parents yet either." Penny sighs, knowing that she probably will not be allowed to go to a party where there are no parents to chaperone. Penny's day is not off to a very good start.

"RRRR-ING! RRR-ING!" The first bell of the day announces class.

"You better ask them soon!" Dianne commands. "I really want you two to be there. I will see you at lunch." Dianne waves good-bye and runs off to her classroom.

As she walks to her classroom, Penny realizes that she forgot to bring her math homework to school. "I cannot believe I forgot it!" Penny says to herself. "Nothing is going right today."

"We are going to do math first," Penny's teacher, Mrs. Davis, announces as she walks up to the blackboard. "Problem number one on the homework was twelve times nine. Penny, will you please tell us the answer?"

Penny does not say anything.

"Penny," Mrs. Davis says, "We are waiting."

"Umm, fifteen?"

The other children in the class laugh.

"I am sorry, Mrs. Davis." Penny's voice is quiet as a whisper. "I forgot my homework."

"Well, Penny," Mrs. Davis says, "I am going to have to give you a zero."

The other children in the class laugh even more. Penny wishes she could hide or yell back, but she looks down at the floor. "Yes, ma'am."

After math, Mrs. Davis announces, "It is time for the history quiz."

Penny feels like kicking something. She forgot to study for the quiz! When she looks at the quiz, Penny gets even more upset. She cannot seem to remember the answers she does know, because she is so angry at herself. Her thoughts are all jumbled up.

At lunch, Dianne makes fun of Penny's new black shoes, which squeak as Penny walks.

"Your feet sound like they are quacking. Quack!" Dianne calls after her. "Duck feet! Rubber duck feet!"

Penny feels so angry, she could scream, but she just walks away.

After lunch, when the children go out for recess, Penny is feeling so angry that she does not want to play any of the games. She is so angry, she wants to scream! She does not. Penny holds her anger inside. She feels her angry feelings grow like a giant bubble.

Penny is very glad when the end of the day comes and she can go home. On her walk from school, Penny tries not to think about how bad her day was. Instead, she looks at the shady green trees and feels the warm sun shine down on her. The more she walks, the better Penny feels. Then she remembers Aunt Rose is visiting today. Penny always has fun with Aunt Rose. She begins to skip. By the time Penny arrives home, she feels a lot less angry.

As Penny opens the front door of her house, Max, her brown and white spotted puppy, jumps all over her. Penny bends down to hug Max and he licks her face. Max's kisses make Penny happy. For the first time that day, she has a big smile on her face. In fact, Penny feels so good that she decides to ask her mom about Dianne's party right away.

Penny finds her mother in the kitchen baking cookies for Aunt Rose's visit. "Mom, Dianne invited me to her birthday party at the ice skating rink next Saturday. Can I go?"

"Who is supervising this party?" Penny's mother asks.

"Well, her parents are going to drop us off, but they are not going to stay," Penny admits.

Her mother shakes her head. "Penny, I am not comfortable with the idea of you going to an unsupervised party at the ice skating rink. I am sorry, honey, but the answer is no."

"I knew you would not let me go! You never let me do anything I want to do!" Penny stamps her feet.

"Penny, you are only nine years old. I do not think you are old enough to go to this party by yourself," Penny's mom says.

"I hate you!" Penny yells. She stomps up the stairs to her bedroom. She slams her bedroom door shut and throws her teddy bear across the room. As the bear hits the wall, one of his button-eyes falls off. Penny begins to cry. Teddy is her favorite toy. Penny has gotten so angry that her head begins to hurt.

Just then, the doorbell rings. Max runs to the door and barks. Penny's mother answers the door. It is Penny's Aunt Rose, visiting from Ohio for a few days. "Where is Penny?" Aunt Rose asks, looking around and putting down her small suitcase.

"She is up in her room. I am afraid Penny is very angry right now. She wants to go to an unsupervised party at the ice skating rink next weekend and I will not let her go."

"Maybe I can speak to her," says Aunt Rose.

"Please do. Penny seems to be very angry lately and she will not talk to me about it." Penny's mom looks sad.

"I will be glad to talk to her. After all, I am a school counselor and I may be able to help Penny sort out her feelings," Aunt Rose replies. She walks up the stairs to Penny's room.

"Penny, it is Aunt Rose. May I come in?" asks Penny's aunt, lightly knocking on the door.

"I do not care!" Penny shouts.

Aunt Rose carefully opens the door and walks into the room. Penny is sitting on her bed with her arms folded. She is so mad that she feels as though smoke is coming out of her ears!

"I am really mad," Penny states. "I am so angry, I could scream!"

"I know and that is good," Aunt Rose says.

"What?" Penny asks with surprise.

"Anger is an important emotion. You need to listen to what your anger is telling you about your feelings. Is the party the only thing about which you are angry?" Aunt Rose asks.

"No," Penny sighs, "there is a lot of other stuff, too."

"Oh, I see," says Aunt Rose. Then she walks to Penny's desk and sits down. She takes some paper and a pen from the drawer. "I think I know a project that will help you feel better."

Penny gets off her bed. She walks over to Aunt Rose and asks, "How will this make me feel better?"

"You will see," Aunt Rose replies. "I am going to make an Anger Chart for you, but I will need your help. First, we make a column titled: 'Things That Make Penny Angry.' The second column we will call: 'Why This Makes Penny Angry.' The third column will be: 'How Penny Can Use Anger In Positive Ways.'

"Now, Penny, I want you to tell me all the things that made you feel angry or upset today and I will write them down."

Penny takes a deep breath. She thinks about her day and begins to speak: "The first thing that got me angry today was all the trash around the schoolyard. I stepped on a rotten apple and almost fell."

Aunt Rose writes down Penny's complaint. "That is a very good thing about which to be angry. The teachers and students at your school should dispose of their trash in the right places," Aunt Rose states. "What else made you angry?"

"My friend, Dianne, is always saying mean things to me. Today, she said my sweater made me look like a rubber duck. At lunchtime, she made fun of my shoes and called me 'rubber duck feet.' Also, I forgot my math homework, so the teacher gave me a zero." Penny's face grows redder as she talks. "After that, we had a history quiz and I messed it up. When I got home, Mom would not let me go to my friend's birthday party," Penny pouts.

"Okay, let us take these problems one at a time," Aunt Rose says. "Why does litter on the school grounds make you so angry?"

"It looks bad and it is not good for the earth," Penny answers sadly. "We should recycle what we can and put the other stuff into garbage cans."

"Is there anything that you can do about recycling at your school? For instance, is there a club to help the environment?" asks Aunt Rose.

"No, there is no club like that," answers Penny.

"Maybe you and your teacher could start one and help promote recycling at your school," Penny's aunt says. Then Aunt Rose writes this down on the Anger Chart.

"You really think I could start a club? Do you think I could make a difference?" asks Penny excitedly.

"Of course you can make a difference!" Aunt Rose offers.

"I will talk to my teacher about starting a club first thing tomorrow," Penny says with a smile.

"Good, Penny. Now, let us talk about your friend, Dianne. I can understand that when she says an unkind thing it bothers you. Have you tried to talk to Dianne? Have you asked her why she says mean things?"

"No, I just keep quiet," replies Penny, "but sometimes I feel so angry, I could scream."

"I see," says Aunt Rose. "Holding things in until you explode is not healthy. However, the way you express your anger is very important. There are good ways and bad ways. The best way to talk to someone with whom you are angry is to use 'I' statements. If you say 'You do this' or 'You do that,' the person usually will get upset. Do you understand?" Aunt Rose asks.

Penny answers, "I think I understand. Instead of saying 'You make me mad when you say mean things to me,' I should say 'I really get upset and angry when you say mean things to me.'"

"Yes, that is good," replies Aunt Rose. "Be even more specific. Perhaps tomorrow you could say to Dianne: 'I am really upset, because yesterday you said my yellow sweater made me look like a rubber duck and you made fun of my shoes. I wish you would not say mean things to me anymore,'" Aunt Rose demonstrates.

"I should tell her exactly what she did to upset me and ask her not to do it again?" asks Penny.

"Yes. It also helps to add what will happen if the person does not stop being mean. You could say, 'If you want to be my friend, you cannot keep saying unkind things to me,'" suggests Aunt Rose.

"Okay, Aunt Rose, I will try it," Penny says and smiles. Aunt Rose smiles, too.

"Now, Penny, what else made you angry today?"

"I forgot to bring in my math homework and I got a zero for the assignment. I also forgot to study for a history quiz."

"How did you feel when you forgot these things?" asks Aunt Rose.

"I felt stupid and angry," Penny says. "I should have remembered to put my homework in my bookbag this morning. I should have remembered to study for the quiz."

"Bringing in your assignments on time and getting good grades are important, Penny, but did anything really awful happen because you forgot your homework? Did the earth blow up? Did the sky fall down?" Aunt Rose laughs.

"No, the earth did not blow up and the sky did not fall down," Penny says with a bigger laugh.

"Good," Aunt Rose says. "Then you learned a valuable lesson. It is normal to make mistakes and forget things once in a while. The important thing is to figure out how to deal with mistakes so they will not be repeated. Now what do you think you can do so you will not forget your homework in the future?"

"Well, I can make sure that I pack my bookbag at night, not in the morning."

"That is an excellent idea, Penny. Another way to help you remember your homework is to keep a notebook with your assignments written in it. Then you can check off each assignment as you complete it. We can go out and buy a new notebook today."

Aunt Rose writes down the suggestions in the correct column on the Anger Chart.

"The notebook will also help me to remember to study for my next history quiz," Penny says. "Then I can get a better grade."

"Good, Penny. You have learned another valuable lesson. Forgive yourself for past mistakes and look ahead," Aunt Rose says. "Now for the big problem, the birthday party!"

"It really makes me angry that Mom thinks I am too young to go without adults being there." Penny frowns.

"Do you think your mom is telling you that you are too young because she does not like you?" Aunt Rose asks.

"No, I know she loves me," Penny says softly.

"I think the best thing you can do is to realize that when you are a child, your parents make the rules. It is not because they hate you, but they are concerned about you," Aunt Rose says.

"Yes, I guess," Penny replies.

"Are you still angry about the party?" Aunt Rose asks.

"A little."

"Sometimes doing something physical like running or playing sports helps to get angry feelings out," explains Aunt Rose.

Penny smiles. "When I was walking home from school I felt better, because I was not thinking about my bad day."

"Exactly. Doing physical exercise helps to get rid of some of the steam building up inside you! What can you do on the day of the party so that you will feel better?" asks Aunt Rose.

"Well, I do not think Patty's parents will let her go to the party, either. Maybe Mom would take us to the movies or we could have a sleepover."

"Those sound like fun ideas!" Aunt Rose tells Penny. "Now, let us look at your Anger Chart together."

PENNY'S ANGER CHART

THINGS THAT MAKE PENNY ANGRY	WHY THIS MAKES PENNY ANGRY	HOW PENNY CAN USE ANGER IN POSITIVE WAYS
There is trash all over the schoolyard.	It looks bad and it is not good for the environment.	1. I can start an environmental club at school. 2. I can talk to teachers and the principal about recycling.
Dianne says mean things to me.	She is supposed to be my friend and friends should not be mean.	1. I should not hold anger in. 2. I should talk to Dianne using "I" statements.
I forgot my math homework.	I got a zero on the assignment and I felt dumb.	1. I should be sure to pack my bookbag the night before. 2. I will remember that it is normal to make mistakes and that it is not the end of the world when I make them.
I did poorly on the history test.	I should have remembered to study for the test.	1. I can copy homework into a notebook and check off each assignment as it is completed. 2. I will look at the big picture: Doing well on my next test will improve my grade.
Mom will not allow me to go to an unchaperoned party.	Mom thinks I am too young to go.	1. I will remember that Mom is not being mean. She loves me and does not want me to get hurt. 2. I will accept that right now my parents are in control. 3. I will do something physical or creative to release anger. 4. I will do something fun the day of the party.

"Thank you for helping me make the Anger Chart. Before you came to my room, I was so angry, I wanted to scream. I was even getting a headache, Aunt Rose. I feel a lot better now that we have talked about my problems," Penny says with a smile.

"I am glad I could help. Penny, remember that you should always listen to your feelings and try to figure out why you are feeling sad or angry. Once you know the reason, you can work on the problem that causes your anger and help yourself feel better," Aunt Rose says.

"Are you ready to shoot some hoops?" Penny asks as she grabs a basketball.

"I sure am! Before we go outside, do you think you should talk to your mom? She was very sad, because you yelled at her," Aunt Rose says.

"I told her I hated her!" Penny says, ashamed. "I did not mean it though. I love her. I was just mad."

"Your mother knows that when people are angry they sometimes say things that they do not mean. However, I am sure that she would feel much better if you tell her what you just told me," Aunt Rose states.

"I will go tell her right now!" Penny goes down the stairs and looks for her mother.

Penny finds her mom in the kitchen, taking cookies out of the oven.

"Mom, I am really sorry that I yelled at you when you told me I could not go to Dianne's party. I do not hate you. I love you very much. Aunt Rose explained to me that you still love me even though you will not let me go to the party," Penny says, as she gives her mom a hug.

"I will always love you very much, no matter what you do or say," her mother replies, smiling.

The next day at school, Penny sees Dianne and Patty. She walks over to them.

"Dianne," Penny says, "yesterday, you made fun of my yellow sweater and my shoes. You called me 'rubber duck feet.' I get really upset when you say those kinds of things."

"I am sorry, Penny. I was joking. I did not think I was being mean to you. I was trying to be your friend."

"Well, I think friends should make each other feel good about themselves and not say mean things to one another."

"Gosh," Dianne says, looking down at the ground. "If my jokes made you mad, I am sorry."

"Thank you," Penny answers. "Instead of saying mean things, we can try to give each other a compliment every day. I will start by giving you one: That pink shirt looks nice. Now you give me a compliment."

"Your hair looks, um, very pretty today," Dianne stammers.

"Thank you. Do you think that is better than being mean to a friend?"

Dianne nods. "Yes, it is better. So, are you two coming to my party on Saturday?" Dianne asks Penny and Patty.

"No, I cannot. My mom thinks I am too young to go to a party unless adults are there," says Penny, frowning.

"My mom said I was too young, too," replies Patty.

"Well, I wish you two could come," Dianne says. "Oh, there is Alice. I will go ask her if she can come to my party. I will see you later." Dianne waves good-bye.

"I cannot believe you finally told Dianne how mean she has been to you," Patty says.

Penny smiles. "I am glad I did. I feel much better. My Aunt Rose is a counselor and she says we should listen to our angry feelings and find ways to deal with them."

"I hope Dianne is nicer to you from now on," Patty says.

Penny nods. "Since we cannot go to Dianne's party, do you want to come over to my house? Maybe we could go to the movies with my mom."

"That sounds like fun," Patty says.

The bell rings. Patty and Penny rush off to class.

Before the start of class, Penny walks up to her teacher. "Mrs. Davis, I want to start a club for recycling and getting rid of trash in our schoolyard."

"That is a wonderful idea, Penny. I will help you," Mrs. Davis says with a smile. Later, when the teacher gives homework assignments, Penny proudly takes out her new notebook and begins to write them down. Penny has begun learning to handle her anger in positive ways. She feels good about herself all day.

When things go wrong, do not let your anger grow and grow. No matter what the problem is, you can deal with it. There is no problem so big that it cannot be worked out.

I hope the next time you feel so angry you could scream that you will take the time to figure out what is wrong. Anger can be a very important feeling, because it tells you something is bothering you. Find an adult with whom to share your angry thoughts and feelings. Together, like Penny and Aunt Rose, you can complete the blank Anger Chart on the next page. You can use the chart to figure out what bothers you and why. Then you can try to find solutions. Once you do, you can take action and change those things that made you angry. You will not be angry anymore, because you will have dealt with your bad feelings in good ways. Like Penny, you will feel good about yourself.

THE END

MY ANGER CHART

THINGS THAT MAKE ME ANGRY	WHY THIS MAKES ME ANGRY	HOW I CAN USE ANGER IN POSITIVE WAYS

MY ANGER CHART

THINGS THAT MAKE ME ANGRY	WHY THIS MAKES ME ANGRY	HOW I CAN USE ANGER IN POSITIVE WAYS

TIPS FOR CHILDREN

1. Listen to your feelings. Your anger is telling you something is not right.

2. Even when you are angry, you are responsible for your actions. Take a deep breath and count to ten before reacting to a situation that is bothering you. Give yourself a chance to calm down. Walk away if you need to and deal with it once you have settled down.

3. Watch your angry words. Penny should not have told her mother that she hates her. She did not really hate her mother. You do not have the right to harm anyone's body, things or feelings.

4. Talk it out—figure out what is upsetting you. Create your own Anger Chart and problem solve.

5. Be a good listener when you are talking a problem out. Have you ever felt like no one was listening to you? It is not a very good feeling. Try to understand how the other person is feeling. Be willing to compromise.

6. If there is a problem at school, do not just ignore it. Talk with a teacher or a counselor. Keep talking with people until it is resolved.

7. When you are angry about something you cannot change or control, work to help yourself. Find something healthy like exercise to do. Penny decided to do something fun on the day of the party that she was not allowed to go to. Try to find a way to bring joy into your life even if it is just for a little while.

8. Make sure you are not lashing out (getting angry with) the wrong person. Sometimes it is easy to take your anger out on your parents or siblings. Getting angry with the wrong person is not going to change the problem. It is just going to create more problems.

9. Say good, kind things to yourself, like *I can work this out. I can make this better.*

10. Use your anger for good. Work toward positive change. Get angry and make this whole world a better place.

TIPS FOR PARENTS AND CAREGIVERS

1. As the adult, it is very important that you stay as calm as possible when your children are angry. Do not match their emotions or you may end up in a screaming match.

2. Remind your child that it is okay to feel angry but it is not okay to hit, throw, bite, etc. Talk it out.

3. It is, however, okay to hit a pillow. But eventually you still have to talk it out.

4. Explain to your child that Penny should not have told her mother that she hates her. We have to all watch our angry words and have self-control. Once hurtful words are said they can't be unsaid. We can however, apologize and try not to do it again.

5. Time-outs to cool down are good for both child and parent. Once everyone is calm, then you can talk about solutions.

6. As a parent or caregiver, it is very important that you role model appropriate ways of handling your anger. Monitor your own yelling. Make sure that you are always in control of your own words and actions.

7. No one is perfect. Sometimes I may manage my anger more poorly than others but I do not hurt anyone, physically or emotionally. If, as a parent, you react badly to something, explain to your child that you want to do better and work on it. It is okay for your children to see that you are also a work in progress. If you feel that you sometimes cross the line with your own anger, seek professional help immediately. End the cycle of abuse in which you may be caught.

8. Children sometimes can be moody because they are tired or not feeling well. Make sure your child gets plenty of sleep. Show your children kindness and understanding. If this is what you feel is happening, find a quiet activity and reassure your children that everything is okay.

9. It can be difficult to be kind to a screaming child who may be spiraling out of control but this child needs your love and guidance. Stay calm and remain the adult.

10. Once the storm has passed and you have talked out the angry feelings, you can form a plan for problem solving. Hug your children. Let your children know that you are always there for them and love them even when they have steam coming out of their ears and feel like screaming!